AF427433

COLD
FEVER
™
-BOOKS-

Beauty Is Skin Deep
by Matt Heart

Beauty Is Skin Deep

by Matt Heart

Published by
Cold Fever Books
P.O Box 8742
Maumee, Ohio 43537
Cover Design by Matt Heart & Lori Heart
Printed in the United States of America
Second Edition: Paperback
November 21, 2024
ISBN:9798230315636
First Edition Paperback
October 24, 2024
ISBN-13 : 979-8343945706
ebook ISBN:9798227691774
ebook ASIN :B0DJZMVK9Y

www.coldfeverbooks.com

Also by Matt Heart

Cold Fever Books
Cold Fever Volume One
Little Red Ridin' in the Hood
Panic at the Drive-in
The Kid Who Talked to Much
Harold Nose Best
Beauty is Skin Deep
Ho Ho Help
Monster Juice
A 10 Minute Decision
The SnowBorn
What's Under My Bed
Zombielicious

Standalone
The Boney Man
Dare to Wake the Dead
Nightmare in a Toy Store
Ash Wednesday

Iniquity
Ding Dong Witch
Tender Eyes
The Incredible Bobbi Myers
Caller Number Seven
Hypoxia

Watch for more at www.coldfeverbooks.com.

Table of Contents

This book is dedicated to my beautiful & glamorous
sister Minnie Foxx

Chapter One:

The Pursuit of Perfection

MINNIE WAS OBSESSED with fashion and beauty. She spent hours online, scrolling through endless beauty blogs, tutorials, and influencer feeds, always in search of the next revolutionary skincare routine or makeup trend. Despite her efforts, she never felt satisfied with her appearance, no matter how much she spent on the latest products. Standing at 5'3", with long reddish-brown hair, green eyes, and pale skin with a soft peach glow, Minnie was naturally beautiful, but she was fixated on achieving more. To her, perfection was always out of reach.

She worked as an editorial executive at one of the top fashion magazines in the bustling city. Her career was a dream come true. Minnie had money, style, and access to all the latest trends, yet she couldn't shake the feeling that something was missing. No matter how much she tried, she never liked what she saw in the mirror.

Walking into the break room one morning, she spotted Deborah sitting at a table with her half-eaten lunch. Deborah smiled politely. "How's your morning?" she asked.

"Not bad, Deb, just have a little headache," Minnie replied, grabbing a mug off the counter and pouring herself some coffee. "Maybe this will wake me up."

Deborah eyed Minnie's face. "You look wonderful today!"

Minnie brightened. "You think so? It's a new makeup I'm trying. I found it online. It's supposed to be all-natural, vegan, and they don't even test it on animals."

"Oh, wow!" Deborah said, sounding impressed as she put her lunch back into the fridge. In truth, Deborah didn't think much of Minnie's makeup, but she always told her boss she looked beautiful—it helped keep things smooth at work.

Minnie smiled, satisfied with the compliment, and left the break room. As she walked back to her office, she opened her compact and checked her face, running her fingers through her soft, flowing hair. Closing the compact, she took a sip of coffee, heading down the hallway back to her desk.

Once in her office, she wandered over to the large window, glancing at the busy street below. Cars and pedestrians moved like ants in the distance, but something caught her eye. Down on the corner was a small shop that looked unfamiliar.

"That's odd," she thought, squinting her eyes. The shop's sign read In the Mix Beauty Shop.

"How have I never noticed that before?" she wondered, intrigued. A beauty shop? Right across the street? She made a mental note to check it out on her way home.

Sitting back at her desk, Minnie flipped through a pile of fashion magazines, scanning articles and tapping away on her computer. The phone rang, snapping her from her thoughts.

"Hey Minnie, can you step into my office for a minute? I need to speak with you," Gerald, the vice president, said on the other end.

"No problem. Be right there," she replied, setting down her coffee.

Minnie walked down the long hallway to the elevator, heading up to the 27th floor. After passing rows of cubicles, she stepped into Gerald's spacious office, where he sat with a few other board members.

"Have a seat, Minnie," Gerald gestured. "We've been talking, and we'd like you to represent us at the upcoming fashion conference next month."

Minnie's eyes widened, and she smiled. "Me? I'd be honored!"

Gerald nodded. "Great. Just make sure you look your best—we're trying to impress a top-tier client." He pulled out the company checkbook and scribbled down a check. "Here, take this. $2,000. Get yourself a new outfit, get your hair done, nails, the works. We want you looking top-notch."

Minnie took the check with a grateful smile. "You got it, Mr. Henderson. Thank you!"

Gerald dismissed her, and she returned to her office, buzzing with excitement. After the workday ended, Minnie grabbed her purse and left the office building, stepping out into the lively city street. The smell of roasted peanuts and bagels filled the air as food vendors lined the sidewalks.

As she walked a block, she remembered the beauty shop she had seen earlier. Curiosity piqued, she made her way toward it.

The door chimed softly as she entered. The shop was small but immaculately decorated, filled with gleaming shelves of beauty products. A stunning woman, about 5'5" with long blonde hair, blue eyes, and perfectly red lips, approached her from behind the counter. Her high cheekbones and elegant figure made Minnie feel plain by comparison.

"Can I help you?" the woman asked with a warm smile.

Minnie was taken aback by her beauty and couldn't help but stare for a moment before regaining her composure. "Yes... um, how long have you been in business? I walk by here all the time, but I've never noticed this shop before."

The woman smiled, her lips curling slightly. "We just opened a week ago."

Minnie nodded. "Wow. It's beautiful in here."

The woman extended her hand. "I'm Rasha, the owner."

"Minnie," she replied, shaking her hand. "Is there anything you can recommend to help me... well, look as good as you?"

Rasha laughed softly. "I think I have just the thing." She reached behind the glass cabinet and pulled out a sleek compact. "Here. A free sample, just for you. Apply it twice a day—once in the morning and once at night. Let me know how it works."

Minnie hesitated, surprised by the offer. "I couldn't... I must pay you for it."

Rasha waved her off with a graceful hand. "No need. It's yours. Consider it a gift."

Minnie accepted the compact with a grateful smile. "Thank you. I'll definitely let you know how it works."

As she left the shop, the excitement of trying the new makeup bubbled within her. She couldn't wait to see what it would do.

Chapter Two:

More

Over the next few days, Minnie noticed an extraordinary change. Her skin became radiant, smooth, and flawless, as though she'd been airbrushed by a professional photographer. Every time she glanced at her reflection, she smiled in awe of her glowing, perfect complexion. The dark circles under her eyes disappeared, and her pores seemed to shrink. She felt like she'd finally found the secret to true beauty.

People around her couldn't help but notice. When she walked into the office, heads turned—especially the men. Every eye seemed to follow her as she strode past cubicles, her confidence growing with every step. The women in the office stared too, but with a mix of curiosity and envy. Minnie relished the attention. She had always been noticed, but never like this. She felt irresistible.

Even when she went grocery shopping or walked down the street, strangers couldn't take their eyes off her. Men stopped in their tracks to watch her, their gazes lingering long after she passed. Women whispered behind her back, casting jealous glances at her flawless face and immaculate makeup. Minnie soaked it all in, loving every second of her newfound allure.

At home, she would stand in front of the mirror, running her hands over her skin. No blemishes, no imperfections—just perfection. She felt like she was finally becoming the woman she had always wanted to be.

But as quickly as the transformation had come, the sample ran out. Minnie found herself scraping the bottom of the compact, trying to get the last bit of the miraculous product. She needed more, and fast. The idea of going a day without it sent a wave of panic through her. The thought of returning to her old self, of losing this new beauty, was unbearable.

That afternoon, she rushed back to In the Mix Beauty Shop. The small bell above the door chimed as she entered. Rasha, as beautiful as ever, looked up from behind the counter and smiled.

"Minnie," she said, her voice smooth and welcoming. "Back so soon? You look incredible."

Minnie smiled, pleased by the compliment. "Thank you. I did exactly as you told me—once in the morning and once at night before bed. It's been amazing. But…" She hesitated, pulling the empty compact from her bag. "I've run out, and I was wondering if I could buy more."

Rasha nodded knowingly. "Of course." She reached behind the glass cabinet and pulled out another compact, identical to the first.

"For you, no problem at all."

Minnie exhaled in relief, grateful that she could continue using the product. "How much?" she asked.

"$50," Rasha replied, her smile never fading.

Minnie paused for a moment, thinking to herself how small a price it was to pay to look this good. $50 for this level of beauty? It was a bargain. Without hesitation, she pulled out her wallet and handed over the cash.

"Thank you," Minnie said, taking the compact with both hands, as if it were a precious treasure.

"Anytime," Rasha said. "Let me know how it continues to work for you."

Minnie left the shop, feeling lighter, happier. With her new compact in hand, she was confident that the beauty she'd achieved wouldn't fade. It was just the beginning.

Chapter Three:

The Cracks Begin to Show

MINNIE FOLLOWED THE same routine religiously. Every morning and every night, she applied the product as Rasha had instructed. Each time, she watched as her reflection in the mirror became more stunning. Her skin was flawless, her eyes sparkled with an unnatural brightness, and her hair seemed to shine even more than before. She had become addicted to the compliments, the way people looked at her with admiration or envy. She couldn't remember the last time she felt so good about herself.

But as the days went on, something started to feel... off.

It began with small things. At first, Minnie noticed that her skin, though beautiful, felt strange under her fingertips—almost too smooth, like the surface of a doll. She brushed it off, thinking it was just a side effect of the product doing its job. But then, her reflection started to play tricks on her. Sometimes, when she looked into the mirror, she swore she saw something—just for a split second. A brief shimmer, a distortion of her features, almost as if the makeup was shifting on her face.

One night, as she sat in front of her vanity, preparing for bed, she saw it again. Her reflection in the mirror wavered, her face flickering as though there was something underneath—something not quite right. She leaned closer to the mirror, heart pounding, but her reflection returned to normal, perfect as ever.

"Just my imagination," she whispered to herself, applying another layer of the product to calm her nerves.

The next morning, Minnie arrived at the office to more compliments. Every man turned his head as she walked by, and even her boss, Gerald, seemed to do a double take as he passed her in the hallway. But this time, the compliments felt hollow. The attention she craved so badly began to feel overwhelming, almost suffocating.

"Looking gorgeous as always, Minnie," Deborah said as they met in the break room. But instead of feeling flattered, Minnie felt uneasy. The way Deborah stared at her didn't feel like admiration—it felt like fear.

When Minnie got back to her office, she sat down at her desk and opened her compact, applying more of the product. She told herself it was just nerves, that everything was fine. But something in her reflection looked different today. Her skin was flawless, yes, but it was too perfect—unnatural, almost plasticky, as if her face were beginning to harden.

She shook her head, closing the compact with a snap. I'm being paranoid, she thought.

But the feeling of something being off grew stronger with each passing day. Every time she walked past a mirror or caught her reflection in a window, she felt a subtle but undeniable change in her appearance. Her features were still beautiful, but they no longer felt like her own.

Then, one evening, as she was getting ready for bed, she noticed something alarming. Her eyes, which had once been a striking green, were changing. At first, it was barely noticeable—a slight tint of yellow in the whites. But now, under the soft glow of the bathroom light, the green in her eyes had deepened, almost glowing unnaturally.

She panicked, staring into the mirror, wondering if it was just a trick of the light. This isn't real. It can't be.

Her heart raced as she reached for the compact, desperately reapplying the product in the hopes that it would fix whatever was happening. As she layered it on, her skin smoothed out, and her eyes returned to normal—for now.

She let out a shaky breath, her hand trembling as she closed the compact. Whatever was happening, she couldn't stop using the product now. She needed it more than ever.

Chapter Four:

Side Effects

THAT MORNING, MINNIE lay in bed, exhausted. She had woken up feeling strange, her body heavy and sluggish, her mind clouded with confusion. Her phone buzzed beside her, and she glanced at the screen—Mom calling. She picked up the phone, her voice groggy.

"Hey, Mom. What's wrong?"

"Honey," her mother's voice came through, warm and familiar. "Why do you say that? I can hear it in your voice—are you okay?"

Minnie rubbed her eyes. "I'm fine, Mom. Just don't feel like myself, I guess."

"Well, I was calling to see what you were doing this weekend. Your father and I are going up to the cabin. We thought you might want to come spend some time with us. Your sister misses you, and I was going to make your favorite lasagna."

Minnie forced a smile, though her mom couldn't see it. "That sounds great. I can be there around 5:00 p.m."

"Perfect!" her mom said, sounding pleased. "See you then, sweetie."

Minnie hung up and tossed the phone onto the bed. She grabbed the TV remote and mindlessly flicked through channels, her stomach churning as she caught glimpses of a movie, a sitcom, and cartoons. Without warning, a wave of nausea hit her hard. Her belly rumbled, and she felt a sudden urge to vomit.

She bolted upright, barely making it to the bathroom in time. She leaned over the toilet, retching violently. When she finally caught her breath, she opened her eyes and froze. The vomit in the toilet was bright green—unnaturally green.

"What the...?" she muttered, horrified.

Minnie stared at the strange liquid, her heart pounding in her chest. Her hands trembled as she rushed to the sink, cupping water in her hands to rinse her mouth. She splashed her face, trying to calm herself, but her mind raced with questions. Could it be food poisoning? She tried to recall what she had eaten the day before but nothing stood out.

She wiped her face with a towel and cautiously glanced back at the toilet. The green vomit glistened under the bathroom light, the color so vibrant it looked almost toxic.

"Maybe I ate something bad..." she whispered to herself, though deep down, she knew that wasn't it.

Trying to shake the unease, Minnie took a shower, hoping it would wash away the discomfort. But as the hot water ran over her skin, she noticed something else. Her reflection in the glass shower door was distorted, like the steam had morphed her appearance. For a split second, her face looked alien—her skin pulled tight, her eyes too large, glowing faintly. She blinked, and the image disappeared.

She stood there, frozen, her mind reeling. What is happening to me?

After her shower, she got ready for work, determined to shake off the strange events. As she walked to the office, her thoughts were plagued by what she had seen. She passed In the Mix Beauty Shop, glancing over her shoulder at the window. The shop was dark, the lights off, the door closed. The strange thing was, she couldn't see anything inside—not a single reflection or shadow. It was as though the shop had vanished, leaving only an empty shell behind.

"Maybe they're not open on Fridays," she thought, trying to brush off the eerie feeling creeping up her spine.

But the feeling didn't leave. As she continued to walk to work, she began to notice things—things that weren't right. Her reflection in passing windows flickered, her face looking almost... wrong. The expressions she saw didn't match what she was feeling. It was like she was looking at someone else's face superimposed on her own.

The air felt thicker as she approached the office building, almost suffocating. She hurried inside, trying to push the unsettling thoughts away. But as she entered the elevator, her hands began to tremble again, a deep sense of dread gnawing at her.

LATER THAT EVENING,

That night, after another exhausting day, Minnie returned home and collapsed onto the couch. Her body felt like it was falling apart—every muscle ached, her head pounded, and the nausea was back with a vengeance. She decided to try and sleep it off.

But as she lay in bed, something terrifying happened.

She woke up in the middle of the night, gasping for breath. The room was cold—unnaturally cold. She reached for her bedside lamp, but her fingers felt numb, as though her hand didn't belong to her. When the light flicked on, she saw it.

Her skin was no longer her own.

Her hands, once soft and peach-colored, were now a sickly gray, the texture rough, like scales. Her veins bulged unnaturally, snaking up her arms, glowing faintly beneath the surface. She stumbled out of bed, running to the bathroom mirror, her heart pounding in terror.

When she looked into the mirror, she screamed.

Her face... it was no longer recognizable. The beautiful, flawless skin she had cherished was gone. In its place was something grotesque. Her skin was tight, stretched unnaturally over sharp bones, her eyes sunken and glowing faintly green. Her hair was falling out in patches, leaving bald spots on her once-perfect head.

She stared at the monster in the mirror, her chest heaving with panic.

"No, no, no!" she cried, clawing at her skin, hoping to tear off whatever this was, but it was no use. The product had changed her—trapped her—in this grotesque form.

As tears streamed down her face, she heard a voice in her mind, a cold, soothing voice.

"You're becoming one of us."

Minnie spun around, but no one was there. She backed away from the mirror, shaking, her reflection watching her with cold, unblinking eyes.

She Screams!

Just as she was about to scream again, she jolted awake.

Minnie sat up in bed, gasping for air, drenched in sweat. Her heart pounded in her chest, the terror of the dream still clinging to her. She looked around the room, disoriented, struggling to remind herself it was just a nightmare.

Her hands trembled as she touched her face. Normal. It's normal.

She jumped out of bed and rushed to the bathroom. Flicking on the light, she stared at her reflection in the mirror, terrified of what she might see. But her face looked the same—her skin flawless, her hair still perfectly in place.

It was just a dream.

Minnie let out a shaky breath, laughing nervously at herself. "Get it together, Minnie," she muttered. "It's just a nightmare."

But as she turned off the light and headed back to bed, a small voice in the back of her mind whispered, What if it wasn't just a dream?

Chapter Five:

The Price of Beauty

THE NEXT MORNING, MINNIE awoke with a sense of dread. Her skin felt tighter than ever, and there was an odd sensation in her jawline—almost as if her bones were shifting beneath the surface. She knew what she had to do. Grabbing her compact, she hurriedly applied another layer of the product, watching as her reflection softened and returned to its flawless state. But deep down, she knew it wasn't enough.

She packed her bag for the weekend at the cabin with her parents and sister. The thought of a quiet weekend away should have filled her with relief, but instead, it only heightened her anxiety. What if the product ran out again while she was away? The thought of losing her beauty—even for a moment—was terrifying.

Minnie made her way back to In the Mix Beauty Shop. As she pushed open the door, the familiar chime rang, and Rasha looked up from behind the counter, her usual knowing smile in place.

"Minnie," Rasha greeted. "Back so soon?"

Minnie hesitated. She didn't want to admit how desperate she was, but there was no hiding it now. "Yes, I need more."

Rasha reached beneath the glass counter, pulling out another compact. But this time, when Minnie asked how much, Rasha's smile widened.

"This time, it's $250."

Minnie blinked, taken aback. The price had increased drastically in such a short time. She hesitated for a moment, feeling a pang of uncertainty. But then she caught her reflection in a nearby mirror, flawless and radiant, and any doubts faded. She couldn't stop now. Not when she had come this far.

Without a second thought, she pulled out her credit card and handed it over. Rasha's eyes gleamed as she processed the transaction.

"You're really starting to fit in," Rasha said cryptically as she handed Minnie the compact.

Minnie's heart skipped a beat at the strange comment, but she brushed it off. "Thanks," she muttered, grabbing the product and leaving the shop.

LATER, AS SHE DROVE toward the cabin, the weight of the past few days began to catch up with her. She felt restless, her thoughts swirling, and decided to call her old friend Rebecca. Maybe a chat would take her mind off things.

After a few rings, Rebecca picked up. "Hey, stranger!" Rebecca's voice was warm and familiar.

There was a pause as Minnie struggled to find the right words. "Sorry... I've just been really busy with work, and I haven't been feeling well lately."

Rebecca's tone softened. "It's okay, I get it. What's up?"

"I'm on my way to the cabin to see my parents for the weekend," Minnie explained. "What about you? What's been going on?"

"Oh, nothing much. Just getting ready to take Jimmy to his first softball game of the summer," Rebecca replied, her voice light. "You should come to one of his games sometime."

Minnie smiled, though a twinge of guilt tugged at her. "I would love to, but I'm going to be out of town for a couple of weeks, so I'm not sure when I'll be able to make it. But I will, eventually. I promise."

In the background, Minnie heard Rebecca's husband calling her. "Come on, honey! We've gotta go."

Rebecca sighed. "Sorry, Minnie, the troop is calling me. We're getting ready to head out right now."

"No problem. I just wanted to catch up."

"Remember, Minnie, we've been best friends since grade school. Life can be crazy, but at the end of the day, we're all we've got. Let's try to stay in touch more."

Minnie felt a pang of nostalgia and nodded, even though Rebecca couldn't see. "You're right. I'll try to call more often."

After they hung up, Minnie turned on the radio, trying to shake off the feeling that she was slipping away from her old life, her old self. A song called My Cereal by Aysha Indigo played, filling the car with a light, carefree vibe. The lyrics caught her attention, and she found herself pondering the words: The moon is 200,000 miles away, you telling me we did it in 3 days? I can't even drive on the overpass without my bucket running out of gas.

She chuckled softly at the absurdity of it, her mind wandering to outer space and how fascinating it would be to visit another planet. But just as quickly as the thought came, her focus shifted back to her own appearance. She couldn't stop thinking about the product, about how it felt like her skin was beginning to betray her. Was it worth it?

She brushed the thought aside as the cabin came into view.

Pulling into the driveway, Minnie saw the familiar glow of her parents' home, nestled in the woods. The lights were on, and the smell of lasagna wafted through the air. Her dad and mom stepped out onto the front porch, smiling and waving as she parked. Her younger sister, Cara, peeked out from behind the window, her face lighting up when she saw Minnie.

Grabbing her bags from the trunk, Minnie walked up the steps, feeling a wave of warmth as her family embraced her. Cara was the first to run out, wrapping her arms around Minnie tightly. Her parents followed, greeting her with smiles and hugs.

"Welcome home, sweetheart!" her dad said, ushering them all inside.

The smell of lasagna filled the air, and Minnie's stomach growled loudly, reminding her of how hungry she was.

"I'm starving," Minnie said with a grin as they made their way into the cozy kitchen.

Cara laughed, leading the way. "Mom's lasagna is as good as ever. You better hurry or Dad might eat it all."

They all gathered around the table, and for a brief moment, Minnie felt a flicker of peace—a welcome distraction from the chaos brewing inside her. But deep down, she knew that the peace wouldn't last.

Chapter Six:

Unraveling

DINNER AT THE CABIN was warm and comforting, just like old times. Minnie sat around the table with her parents and Cara, laughing and swapping stories. Her mother had made lasagna just as promised, and the scent of garlic and cheese filled the room. Everyone was in high spirits, enjoying each other's company. For a brief moment, Minnie felt like she could relax.

As her mother cleared the dishes, she brought out an old board game they hadn't played in years. The family gathered around the table, laughing and joking as they rolled dice and moved pieces across the board. But while everyone else was enjoying the moment, Minnie couldn't shake the unsettling feeling building inside her.

Her stomach churned, and her skin felt tighter than usual, as though it were stretched too thin. A dull ache throbbed at the base of her skull, and the room began to spin slightly. She didn't want to alarm her family, so she forced a smile and excused herself.

"I'll be right back," she said, standing up from the table. "Just need to use the bathroom."

Her family nodded, too engrossed in the game to notice anything was wrong.

In the bathroom, Minnie leaned against the sink, her hands gripping the edges of the countertop. She stared at herself in the mirror, her reflection showing the same flawless face she'd grown used to, but something still felt wrong. Desperately wrong.

She grabbed a paper cup, filling it with water to take a drink, hoping it would settle her stomach. But as she brought the cup to her lips, she felt an unnatural sensation in her mouth. Her eyes widened in horror as she watched a large, gray tongue suddenly flop out of her mouth and into the sink with a sickening slap.

Minnie gasped, dropping the cup, her heart racing. The tongue looked... wrong. It was long, dark, and alien, something that didn't belong to her. She reached out with shaking hands and tried to pull at it, but it flipped back into her mouth just as quickly as it had appeared. She stood there, breathless, gripping the edge of the sink, horrified.

This can't be happening. I'm losing my mind.

She took a few deep breaths, trying to calm herself, and splashed cold water on her face. When she looked up again, her reflection was normal. No tongue. No changes. Just her usual, perfect self.

Minnie shook her head and hurried back to the table, trying to act like nothing had happened. Her heart was still racing, and her mind was filled with panic, but she forced a calm expression.

When she sat down, Cara gave her a curious look. "You okay?"

Minnie nodded quickly. "Yeah, I'm fine. Just tired."

Her father glanced at her, concern in his eyes. "Do you want to turn in for the night, sweetie? You had a long drive."

Minnie smiled weakly. "Yeah, I think I will. I'm just really exhausted."

"Do you want me to tuck you in?" her father teased, trying to lighten the mood.

Minnie laughed softly. "No, Dad, I'm fine. I'll see you in the morning."

She excused herself from the table, and her family nodded in understanding. As she walked down the hallway toward the bedroom, the strange sensation in her mouth lingered. She couldn't shake the feeling that something inside her was changing—and fast.

LATER THAT NIGHT:

As Minnie got dressed for bed, pulling on her nightgown, she felt a sense of relief. The drive, the product, the strange events—it was all catching up to her. She thought maybe she just needed sleep, and everything would be back to normal in the morning. But deep down, she wasn't so sure.

She was facing away from the door when she heard soft footsteps in the hallway. It was Cara. "Minnie?" Cara called softly.

Minnie turned, startled. "Hey, what's up?"

"I just wanted to say goodnight," Cara replied with a smile.

But before she could step into the room, Cara froze in place. For a split second, her eyes widened in confusion. She blinked twice, trying to focus. She had seen something—humps, small, uneven rows of bumps on Minnie's back beneath the fabric of her nightgown.

Cara rubbed her eyes, but when she looked again, the humps were gone. Must be my imagination, she thought, shaking her head.

Minnie noticed the strange look on her sister's face and frowned. "You okay?"

Cara quickly smiled, brushing off the moment. "Yeah, I'm fine. Just tired, I guess. Anyway, goodnight."

The two sisters hugged, and Minnie smiled as Cara left the room. But the unease lingered, growing stronger by the second. Minnie crawled into bed, pulling the covers up to her chin. She closed her eyes, hoping that sleep would come quickly and wash away the day's strangeness.

THE NIGHTMARE BEGINS:

That night, Minnie was pulled into another vivid nightmare. She found herself standing in a dark, endless room. There were no walls, no windows—just an infinite black space. The air was cold, and she could hear a faint buzzing, like insects swarming nearby.

She looked down and saw her reflection in a puddle at her feet. Her face, once flawless and perfect, was now hideously deformed. The skin on her face had split apart, revealing something gray and scaly beneath it. Her hair had fallen out in chunks, leaving her scalp patchy and raw.

She screamed, but no sound came out.

Suddenly, she felt the same unnatural sensation in her mouth. Her tongue—a long, gray, grotesque thing—slithered out and fell into the puddle below. It writhed like a snake, and

Minnie tried to pull it back, but her hands were no longer her own. Her fingers had turned into sharp, bony claws, and her reflection grinned at her, mocking her horror.

"You're becoming one of us," a voice echoed in the darkness.

Minnie stumbled backward, her heart racing. She tried to run, but the black space around her seemed to stretch endlessly, trapping her.

She was no longer human.

The nightmare closed in on her, suffocating and terrifying her.

She wakes up:

Minnie woke up with a gasp, her heart pounding, drenched in sweat. Her hands flew to her mouth, but everything felt normal. Her tongue was... human again.

It had been just a dream.

But as she lay there in the dark, shaking, the sensation of the gray tongue and, making her wonder if the nightmare was more real than she wanted to admit.

Chapter Seven:

The Price of Betrayal

THE WEEKEND AT THE cabin had come to a close, and despite the odd sensations she'd been experiencing, Minnie felt a sense of calm around her family. But now, back at home, reality was sinking in. She had a major conference coming up, and she needed to look perfect. As she unpacked her bag, Minnie realized something was missing—her compact. Panic set in.

Frantically, she searched her room, tearing through her luggage and rifling through the bathroom drawers. Where is it? Her heart pounded in her chest. Without the compact, she couldn't maintain her appearance, and her skin was already beginning to feel tight again. She had no choice but to call her parents.

"Mom? Did I leave my compact at the cabin?" Minnie asked, trying to keep the desperation out of her voice.

Her mother sounded puzzled. "I don't think so, sweetie. Let me ask your father and Cara."

Minnie could hear her mother calling to them, asking if anyone had seen the compact. There was a pause before her mother's voice returned. "Cara has it, honey."

Minnie's stomach twisted in anger. Cara has it?

"What do you mean Cara has it?" Minnie snapped. "Why would she take my things?"

"She said it was a really pretty case, and she didn't think you'd mind. She mentioned you had two of them," her mother explained carefully, trying to calm the tension.

Furious, Minnie clenched the phone tighter. "She didn't ask! She just took it!"

Her mother sighed. "I know, sweetie. I'll have her bring it back, or I can mail it to you if you need it."

But Minnie couldn't wait. The conference was in just two days, and she couldn't risk looking anything less than perfect. She had to have another compact—now. Driving back to the cabin was out of the question; it was over three hours away, and there wasn't enough time.

With a heavy heart, she called Cara directly. Her sister answered with a casual, "Hey, what's up?"

"You took my compact," Minnie said, her voice sharp.

There was a pause. "Oh, yeah. Sorry about that. It's such a pretty case, and I didn't think you'd mind if I borrowed it."

"Don't ever steal from me again, Cara!" Minnie's voice trembled with anger.

"Steal?" Cara sounded offended. "I didn't steal it, Minnie. I just borrowed it. You can have it back."

Minnie was livid. "You don't just take people's things without asking. That's stealing."

Before Cara could respond, Minnie hung up, shaking with fury. She was beyond frustrated. Of all the things to take!

Back at the cabin, Cara stood with the compact in her hand, confused by Minnie's overreaction. Her father walked into the room, raising an eyebrow when he saw her holding the sleek makeup case. "Is that your sister's?" he asked.

"Yeah," Cara said, rolling her eyes. "I just borrowed it. I didn't think it was a big deal."

Her dad frowned. "You really shouldn't take her things without asking, sweetie. But I have to say, you look gorgeous tonight."

Cara's cheeks flushed. "Thanks, Dad. I guess this stuff works pretty well."

Her mother walked in, catching the last part of the conversation. "Wow, Cara, you do look stunning. I might have to try some of that makeup myself."

***BACK IN THE CITY, MINNIE** makes a decision:*

Minnie's heart raced as she threw on her coat and grabbed her car keys. She had no choice but to go back to In the Mix Beauty Shop. She couldn't risk showing up to the conference looking anything less than flawless. The thought of her skin cracking, her features distorting—it was too much to bear.

As she approached the shop, something seemed off. The lights were off, and a sign on the door read Closed. Panic washed over her. No, not now! I need this!

She hesitated for a moment but noticed the door was slightly ajar. Curiosity—and desperation—got the better of her. She gently pushed the door open, peeking her head inside.

"Hello?" she called out. "Is anyone here?"

No one answered. The shop was eerily quiet, the air thick with an odd stillness. But the compacts—her compacts—were just behind the glass cabinet. She couldn't leave without them.

Her heels clicked softly on the floor as she walked toward the back of the shop. The cabinet stood before her, gleaming under the dim light. She crouched down and pulled open the glass door, reaching inside to grab what she needed.

But as she did, something caught her eye. Behind the cabinet, a strange control panel was embedded into the wall. It didn't belong in a beauty shop. Minnie's brow furrowed as she inspected it, her fingers brushing over the unfamiliar buttons and dials.

What is this for? she thought, feeling a sudden sense of unease. The setup looked more like the controls of a machine than anything related to makeup. She glanced around the shop, half-expecting someone to pop out and explain, but the place remained empty.

Brushing off her concerns, Minnie grabbed four compacts from the cabinet and quickly rose to her feet. She couldn't leave without paying, even if no one was there. She dug into her purse and pulled out the check that Mr. Henderson had given her—a generous $2,000.

She signed it over to Rasha and placed it on the counter, leaving a brief note: Your door was open. No one was here, so I helped myself. Sorry. I left some money.

With her mission complete, she hurried out of the shop, the door creaking as she pulled it closed behind her. Her heart pounded as she climbed into her car, the eerie quiet of the shop still lingering in her mind.

As she drove away, her mind raced. What was that control panel? Why did the shop feel so... wrong? But no matter how many questions gnawed at her, Minnie brushed them aside. All that mattered was that she had the product, and she was ready for the conference.

She couldn't afford to think about anything else.

Chapter Eight:

The Glimpse of Horror

MINNIE ARRIVED AT THE conference, trying her best to put the strange events of the past few days out of her mind. She was dressed in a sleek, elegant outfit, her makeup flawless—thanks to the compacts she had taken from the shop. The confidence she used to feel was starting to return, and for a brief moment, she allowed herself to relax.

The large banquet hall was filled with the glittering elite of the fashion world—designers, editors, influencers, and executives mingling together, their laughter and chatter filling the air. Minnie moved through the crowd, clinking glasses with her fellow professionals and sipping her wine, soaking in the atmosphere. This was the world she belonged to. This was the world she had worked so hard to be a part of.

Conversations flowed around her—talk of upcoming collections, trends, and partnerships. Minnie smiled and nodded, engaging where she could, but there was a nagging tension at the back of her mind. She felt off somehow. Her skin still felt too tight, and there was a strange sensation in her face, like it was stretching and contracting all at once. But each time she excused herself to check in a mirror, her reflection looked perfect.

She convinced herself it was just stress.

After the keynote presentation, the room quieted as the next speaker was introduced. The host stood at the podium, beaming as she spoke. "Now, it's my pleasure to introduce one of our own, a visionary in the world of fashion media. Please welcome Minnie Daniels!"

The applause was thunderous as Minnie was ushered onto the stage. Her heart raced, but she kept her composure, flashing a bright smile as she took her place behind the podium. This was her moment. She couldn't let anything go wrong.

As she began to speak, the audience was captivated by her presence, hanging onto every word. She spoke confidently about the future of fashion media, about innovation, about embracing change—everything she had worked so hard to achieve. But as she continued, something began to feel very wrong.

The light above her was hot, unbearably hot, and suddenly, she felt her skin shifting beneath her makeup. Her voice faltered for a moment, but she recovered quickly, brushing it off. It's just nerves, she thought. She pressed on, determined to get through her speech.

But then it happened.

A murmur rippled through the crowd. People were leaning forward, squinting at her, whispering to each other in confusion. Minnie kept talking, but she could feel their eyes on her—really on her. And then she caught a glimpse of herself in the large screen monitor to her right. Her heart stopped.

For a split second, her reflection was hideous. Her once-perfect skin was peeling, revealing patches of scaly, gray flesh underneath. Her eyes, once bright and clear, had turned a sickly yellow, glowing faintly under the stage lights. Her mouth twisted into a grotesque grin, her teeth sharp and uneven. She was a monster.

Minnie gasped, stumbling backward, her hand flying to her face. But when she looked again—she was normal. Flawless. As if nothing had happened.

She quickly composed herself, forcing a smile as the whispers in the audience grew louder. "Excuse me," she said into the microphone, her voice shaky. "I think the lights are playing tricks on us."

Laughter erupted from the crowd, but it was nervous, uncertain. People glanced around at each other, whispering, exchanging confused looks. Some rubbed their eyes as if they had been seeing things.

"Too much wine," one man joked from the front row, and the audience erupted in nervous laughter again.

Minnie forced a laugh, but her heart was still racing. She hurried through the rest of her speech, doing her best to regain control of the room. But even as she spoke, she could feel the weight of their eyes on her. They had seen something—something real.

As she finished, the applause was polite but subdued. Minnie nodded quickly and stepped off the stage, avoiding eye contact as she made her way out of the room. The crowd was still buzzing with confusion, but no one stopped her.

Her hands trembled as she left the banquet hall and found herself alone in a quiet hallway. She leaned against the wall, her breath coming in short gasps. What had just happened? Was it real? Or was it all in her mind?

She looked down at her hands—they were normal. Everything was normal. But the memory of her distorted reflection wouldn't leave her.

For the first time, Minnie felt true terror

Chapter Nine:

The Descent into Isolation

MINNIE SAT IN HER HOTEL room, still reeling from the strange event at the conference. Her hands were shaking as she tried to process what had happened—how everyone had seen her, even if just for a moment. Her phone rang suddenly, jolting her out of her thoughts. It was Mr. Henderson.

She hesitated for a moment before answering. "Hello, Mr. Henderson."

"Minnie!" he said, his voice brimming with excitement. "I just got a phone call. We landed the contract! Did you hear me? I said we landed the contract!"

Minnie's stomach churned, but she forced a smile. "I'm glad I could help."

"Help?" Mr. Henderson laughed. "You did more than help! I'm thinking of promoting you! Desmond, the owner of Clever Fashion, said you pulled off some kind of Halloween trickery during your speech. He swore you looked like a monster for a minute and then turned back! Everyone was laughing by the end of it. Whatever you did, it worked!"

Minnie's heart sank. Her worst fear was confirmed—they had seen her. It wasn't just in my head. She gasped, trying to keep herself calm, but the reality of what happened began to close in on her.

"I— I'm sorry, Mr. Henderson, I have to go," she stammered, her voice shaky.

"Go? Well, okay, but I want you in the office first thing Monday morning," he said, still laughing. "We need to talk about your new promotion! You did a fantastic job, Minnie. I don't know how you pulled it off, but I'll see you Monday."

Minnie barely heard the rest of what he said. She hung up quickly, her mind racing. The call should have been good news, but all she could think about was that everyone had seen her transformation. Desmond had called it a trick, but she knew it wasn't.

She felt sick to her stomach.

Without wasting another moment, she threw her belongings into her suitcase and hurried to check out of the hotel. She booked the first available flight home, desperate to leave the conference behind. The buzzing noise of the hotel lobby, the laughter, the conversations—it all felt like it was closing in on her. She needed to escape.

ON THE PLANE:

Minnie's hands trembled as she sat in the airplane seat, staring blankly out the window. The flight attendants moved down the aisles, offering drinks and snacks, but she ignored them. Her mind was a whirlwind of fear and confusion.

As the plane settled into its cruise altitude, Minnie felt a strange sensation in her eyes. Her vision blurred slightly, and she rubbed her eyelids, trying to clear them. But the irritation grew worse. It felt like something was crawling beneath her skin.

Panicked, she excused herself and made her way to the tiny airplane bathroom. She locked the door behind her and stared into the mirror, her heart racing. Her reflection seemed normal at first glance, but as she leaned closer, she saw something horrifying.

From the corner of her right eye, a tiny worm-like creature wriggled its way out from beneath her eyelid. Minnie froze, watching in shock as it slithered down her cheek and fell into the sink with a soft plop. Her breath caught in her throat.

She gripped the sides of the sink, staring down at the worm as it wriggled for a moment before going still. *This isn't real. This can't be happening.*

Her hands trembled as she splashed water on her face, desperately trying to compose herself. But the sight of the worm was burned into her mind, and no amount of water could wash away the horror of what she had just witnessed.

Minnie stumbled back to her seat, her mind spinning. She felt trapped, suffocated by her own body. She tried to focus on the hum of the plane's engines, but her thoughts raced uncontrollably. *What was happening to her? Was she falling apart?*

The rest of the flight was a blur. All she could think about was getting home.

BACK HOME:

The moment Minnie stepped into her apartment, she locked the door behind her and collapsed onto the couch. Her heart pounded in her chest, her hands shaking uncontrollably. She tried to breathe deeply, but the panic wouldn't go away. I'm falling apart.

She reached for her phone and saw that Mr. Henderson had already called her again. She couldn't bring herself to answer. She couldn't face anyone right now.

For the next few days, Minnie withdrew from everything and everyone. She didn't leave her apartment. She didn't return Mr. Henderson's calls, despite the numerous voicemails he left, each one more urgent than the last.

"Hey, Minnie, it's Mr. Henderson again. I've been trying to reach you for days. We need to talk about your promotion and the conference. Please call me back as soon as you can."

She listened to each message but never replied. The world outside her apartment felt too dangerous, too foreign. She couldn't let anyone see her. She couldn't bear the thought of anyone witnessing what was happening to her.

Her phone buzzed again. Another voicemail. Another message from a friend asking where she had been, why she wasn't answering. But she couldn't deal with them either. Not her friends, not her family—no one.

Minnie spent her days avoiding mirrors, avoiding her reflection. She refused to check her face for fear of what she might see. She felt like she was slowly losing herself, bit by bit, but she didn't know how to stop it.

AS THE DAYS PASSED, her body continued to feel foreign, as if it no longer belonged to her. The transformations were coming more frequently now, brief flashes of her monstrous form appearing in the mirror when she least expected it. Her once-beautiful skin was tightening, cracking, and no matter how much makeup she applied, it could no longer mask what was happening beneath the surface.

She had become a prisoner in her own body, isolated and terrified.

And she had no idea what to do next.

Chapter Ten:

The Metamorphosis

MINNIE STOOD IN HER dimly lit bathroom, staring at the compacts she had taken from the shop. Her hands trembled as she opened them one by one, scraping out every last bit of the precious powder. Desperation had taken hold of her—she was unraveling, her once-beautiful body now something foreign and grotesque. She couldn't stand it anymore. She had to fix it, no matter what it took.

With shaking hands, she emptied the contents of each compact into a bowl, scraping the edges to get every speck of the product. She added water, stirring it into a thick, creamy paste. It shimmered slightly under the dim light, almost glowing, like something otherworldly.

This has to work, she thought. This will fix me.

Minnie began to slather the paste onto her skin, rubbing it over every inch of her body. She started with her feet, carefully spreading it between her toes, making sure to cover every part of her skin. The cool sensation of the product soothed her nerves as she worked her way up her legs, coating her calves and thighs. She moved to her arms, rubbing the thick mixture over her hands and fingers, making sure not to miss a spot.

Her breathing quickened as she lathered the paste over her chest, her back, her neck—anywhere she could reach. She slathered it thickly onto her face, rubbing it in as deeply as she could, hoping the thick layer would mask whatever was wrong with her.

She even smeared it into her hair, massaging the paste into her scalp, desperate to stop the creeping sensation that something was changing beneath the surface of her skin. *If I cover myself completely, it'll stop.*

She rubbed it on thicker and thicker, making sure to leave no part of her body uncovered. The paste felt cold and heavy on her skin, but she didn't care. She needed this. *This will make me beautiful again.*

When she had finally covered herself completely, Minnie stood for a moment, looking at her reflection in the bathroom mirror. She was unrecognizable, a thick layer of creamy substance covering every inch of her skin. She looked like a statue made of porcelain, frozen and fragile. Her body trembled with exhaustion, her muscles aching from the effort.

Satisfied, she stumbled into her bedroom, collapsing onto the bed, her limbs heavy with fatigue. The weight of the paste was like a blanket, pulling her deeper into the mattress. Her eyes fluttered closed, her breathing slowing as she drifted off to sleep.

THE NIGHTMARE:

Minnie fell into a deep, disturbing sleep. In her dream, she was crawling on the ground like a worm, her body small and weak, squirming through the dirt. The world around her was dark and vast, the ground cold and unyielding beneath her. She moved slowly, inching forward, her body writhing as if she were no longer human.

Suddenly, a huge bird swooped down from the sky, its massive wings casting a shadow over her tiny form. Minnie tried to scream, but no sound came out. The bird's beak snapped around her, lifting her from the ground, its sharp edges digging into her soft, fragile body.

She felt weightless as the bird carried her higher and higher, the ground disappearing beneath her. The world spun, and Minnie felt herself being tossed, helpless in the bird's grip. Then, in an instant, she was falling—plummeting toward the earth, spinning uncontrollably through the air.

The sensation shifted, and suddenly Minnie was no longer falling. She was standing in a dark, damp space, surrounded by buzzing noises. She looked down and saw that her hands had changed—they were no longer hands, but sharp claws. Her mouth watered as she realized what she was holding: bugs. Hundreds of wriggling, crawling insects, squirming in her hands.

Without hesitation, she began to eat them, her jaws working furiously as she devoured the bugs. The taste was repulsive, but she couldn't stop. She was consumed by hunger, driven by an insatiable need to consume every last one of them.

The nightmare twisted and warped around her, the buzzing growing louder and louder, until it was all she could hear.

OUTSIDE THE DREAM:

While Minnie dreamed, her body was undergoing a terrifying transformation. The paste she had lathered onto her skin began to harden, drying quickly and forming a thick, shell-like covering. Her skin, once soft and pliable, was now stiff and brittle, cracking in places as the substance dried.

Her entire body was encased in the hardened shell, a cocoon that enveloped her from head to toe. Beneath the surface, her skin continued to change—becoming rough, leathery, and alien. Her muscles twitched involuntarily, as if they were moving on their own, growing and shifting beneath the shell.

Her fingers curled into claws, her nails sharpening to fine points. Her tongue, once human, lengthened and thickened, coiling inside her mouth like a snake. Her back arched as her spine lengthened, bumps forming beneath her skin as if something were trying to break free.

Minnie's body was no longer her own. She was undergoing a metamorphosis, her human form fading away, replaced by something monstrous.

But she was unaware of what was happening. She lay in her bed, trapped inside the hard shell, her body completely immobilized. Inside, she was still. Her breathing was shallow, her heart barely beating. She was in a state of suspension, like a moth in a cocoon, waiting to emerge.

IN THE QUIET OF HER apartment, the air was still. Minnie lay lifeless, her body encased in the thick, hardened shell. The room was dark, and the only sound was the faint creaking of her transforming body as it continued to shift beneath the surface.

She was no longer Minnie Daniels. She was something else. Something monstrous.

Chapter Eleven:

The Transformation Complete

MINNIE STIRRED IN HER bed, feeling a tightness surrounding her body. She tried to move, but something heavy and brittle held her in place. She blinked, disoriented, her breath shallow. It was then that she realized the nightmare hadn't ended—her body was encased in a hardened shell, its surface cold and cracked.

As she shifted, the shell began to splinter, the cracks spreading across the surface like a spiderweb. Piece by piece, it started to fall away, chunks of the shell dropping to the floor with a sickening wet plop, sticky with slime. Minnie's heart pounded as she tried to tear at the pieces, using her hands—now six-fingered, clawed monstrosities—to pull the remnants of the shell off her body.

She gasped in horror as more of the shell fell away, revealing the grotesque form underneath. Her legs were thin and elongated, her back hunched, and her skin a mottled, grayish-green, slick with a strange fluid. She felt the weight of her long, snake-like tongue hanging from her mouth, and her fingers—those sharp, clawed fingers—twitched with an unnatural stiffness.

Minnie stumbled out of bed, pulling the last pieces of the shell off her arms, feeling the cool air hit her new skin. Every step felt foreign, her body unrecognizable. She staggered over to the vanity, needing to see for herself. The mirror was fogged from her breath, but as she wiped it clean, the image staring back at her was worse than any nightmare.

Her reflection was monstrous.

Her face, once beautiful and flawless, was now distorted beyond recognition. Her eyes glowed faintly, a sickly yellow, and her skin, which had once been smooth and radiant, was now leathery and rough, like the surface of an ancient stone. Her mouth—twisted into a gruesome grin by the weight of her elongated tongue—barely resembled anything human.

This can't be happening. She brought her claws up to her face, running them along the sharp, uneven contours of her features. *What have I become?*

Tears welled in her eyes as she realized the full horror of her transformation. *I need to go to the shop. I need answers.*

Minnie rushed to her closet, pulling out a large fedora hat, a thick scarf, and a long black trench coat. She covered her disfigured body as best as she could, hiding her grotesque form beneath the heavy fabric. She knew she couldn't let anyone see her like this.

With trembling hands, she grabbed her car keys and hurried out of her apartment, praying that the darkness of the night would shield her from prying eyes.

AT THE SHOP:

The drive to In the Mix Beauty Shop felt endless. Minnie's mind raced, consumed by fear and confusion. What had Rasha done to her? Why had she been transformed into this... thing? She needed answers. She needed to know why this was happening.

When she arrived at the shop, the lights were off, just as they had been the last time. But the door was slightly ajar again, inviting her in. Minnie hesitated for a moment, her heart pounding in her chest. She took a deep breath, pulling her hat lower over her face, and stepped inside.

The familiar chime of the doorbell rang as she entered. The shop was eerily quiet, but a moment later, Rasha emerged from the back of the building, a wide, knowing smile on her face.

"Minnie... is that you?" Rasha's voice was soft, almost comforting.

Minnie froze, her body trembling under the weight of the trench coat. She hesitated, but Rasha's smile never wavered.

"Let me see you, Minnie," Rasha coaxed, her voice dripping with curiosity. "I've been waiting."

With a deep, shuddering breath, Minnie reached up and slowly removed her hat. Then, the scarf. Finally, with a trembling hand, she pulled off the trench coat, revealing her monstrous form in full. Her twisted figure stood hunched in the dim light, her long, slithering tongue hanging from her mouth.

"What have you done to me?" Minnie cried, her voice hoarse and garbled. Tears streamed down her face, mixing with the thick slime that clung to her skin. "Why did you do this?"

Rasha's eyes glimmered with satisfaction as she stepped closer, her smile widening. "Yes... yes, indeed. You look beautiful," she said with a gleam in her eye, tilting her head to the side. "You've become everything you were meant to be."

Minnie shook her head violently, her claws trembling. "This... this can't be! You did this to me! You tricked me!"

Rasha's smile didn't falter. Instead, she closed her eyes briefly, and when she opened them again, her own skin began to crack. The perfect, human appearance she had worn so easily began to split open, revealing the truth underneath. Her skin peeled back, and as it did, Minnie's eyes widened in horror.

Rasha's true form was alien, just like Minnie's. Her skin was dark and leathery, her eyes glowing a deep, vibrant yellow. She stood taller now, more imposing, her once human face twisted into something otherworldly.

"You're one of us now," Rasha said calmly, her voice no longer soft, but filled with a strange, alien resonance. "This is who you've always been."

As Rasha spoke, the glass cabinet at the back of the shop began to slide open, revealing a control panel hidden within the floor. Lights blinked and flickered, and the walls of the shop began to hum with energy. Minnie's breath quickened as she realized what was happening.

"This... this isn't a shop, is it?" Minnie whispered, her voice trembling.

Rasha smiled darkly. "No, Minnie. It's not. It's a spaceship."

With a swift movement, Rasha walked over to the control panel, pressing a series of buttons. The floor vibrated beneath Minnie's feet as the entire building seemed to shift. Rasha flicked a lever, and with a low hum, a door at the back of the shop slid open.

From the darkness beyond the door, more aliens emerged, each one grotesque and twisted like Minnie. They moved toward her, their eyes gleaming with a strange,

welcoming warmth.

"You've been chosen," Rasha said softly, her voice filled with pride. "You were always meant to be one of us. Welcome home."

Minnie's heart pounded in her chest as she took in the horrifying sight before her. She stumbled backward, tears streaming down her face. "No... no, this can't be..."

But Rasha's smile never wavered. With one final push of a button, the entire building began to lift off the ground, rising higher and higher into the night sky. The city below grew smaller as the shop-turned-spaceship disappeared into the clouds.

As they ascended into the stars, Minnie's last, desperate scream echoed through the ship, fading into the vast emptiness of space.

And if you listened closely, as the spaceship vanished into the night, you could still hear the faint scream of Minnie, lost forever to the void.

THE END

If you enjoyed this book, I invite you to terrorize yourself with the rest of the Cold Fever Books collection. The story doesn't stop here—immerse yourself in even more chilling tales.

Pick up these spine-tingling titles:
A Nightmare in a Toy Store
Zombielicious
The Mystery of Old Oak Inn
Dare to Wake the Dead
Little Red Ridin' in The Hood
The Kid Who Talked Too Much
Panic at the Drive-In
Harold Nose Best

THESE STORIES ARE SURE to terrify you. Grab one now, and read it with your friends—maybe at a sleepover or around a campfire. They're short, sweet, and guaranteed to deliver a good scare.

Scare you later,
Matt Heart

Don't miss out!

Visit the website below and you can sign up to receive emails whenever Matt Heart publishes a new book. There's no charge and no obligation.

https://books2read.com/r/B-A-QPSNC-ORMCF

BOOKS 2 READ

Connecting independent readers to independent writers.

Did you love *Beauty is Skin Deep*? Then you should read *Harold Nose Best*[1] by Matt Heart!

There's something off about the circus that's appeared overnight, and Harold Clemens is at the center of it. Once a beloved entertainer, Harold now has a much darker purpose. Children are drawn to his tent by the sweet scent of popcorn and candy, but not all make it out the same. What Harold is looking for, only he knows. But beware—he's still searching.

In Harold Nose Best, one thing is certain: no one is safe, and everyone has something to lose.

Read more at www.coldfeverbooks.com.

---

1. https://books2read.com/u/38l01w

2. https://books2read.com/u/38l01w

Also by Matt Heart

Cold Fever Books
Cold Fever Volume One
Little Red Ridin' in the Hood
Panic at the Drive-in
The Kid Who Talked to Much
Harold Nose Best
Beauty is Skin Deep
Ho Ho Help
Monster Juice
A 10 Minute Decision
The SnowBorn
What's Under My Bed
Zombielicious

Standalone
The Boney Man
Dare to Wake the Dead
Nightmare in a Toy Store
Ash Wednesday

Iniquity
Ding Dong Witch
Tender Eyes
The Incredible Bobbi Myers
Caller Number Seven
Hypoxia

About the Author

Matt Heart *is a BMA award-winning international singer-songwriter and storyteller whose work bridges the worlds of music and literature. As the founder of 424 Records, Matt has penned over 50 original songs, weaving powerful narratives that explore themes of love, loss, temptation, and self-discovery. His lyrics, much like his books, carry emotional depth and raw authenticity.*

In addition to his musical legacy, Matt is the creator of Cold Fever Books, a chilling literary brand that includes both supernatural crime thrillers and eerie children's horror stories inspired by classics like Goosebumps. His adult novels—Ding Dong Witch, The Boney Man, Iniquity, Tender Eyes, Ash Wednesday, and The Incredible Bobbi Myers—blend psychological tension with the uncanny, while his middle-grade titles, including The Boy Who

Talked Too Much, Zombielicious, Dare to Wake the Dead, Little Red Ridin' in the Hood, and *Nightmare in a Toy Store,* spark young imaginations with spooky fun.

A natural storyteller with a cinematic voice, Matt's work continues to evolve across mediums. Whether crafting a heart-stopping plot twist or a soul-stirring song, he invites his audience into deeply immersive worlds where anything is possible—and nothing is ever as it seems.

To follow Matt's latest releases, music, and projects, visit www.facebook.com/MattHeartFanpage or follow him on X @MattHeart.

Read more at www.coldfeverbooks.com.